أطفال لِر

أسطورة كِلتيّة

The Children of Lir

A Celtic Legend

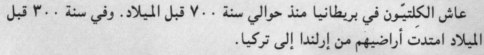

عاش الكلتيّون في بريطانيا منذ حوالي سنة ٧٠٠ قبل الميلاد. وفي سنة ٣٠٠ قبل
الميلاد امتدت أراضيهم من إرلندا إلى تركيا.
كان الكلتيّون الذين ينتمون إلى الجزر البريطانية معروفين بحبهم لسرد القصص.
واستمرت قصص الملك لر وعائلته، الذين كانوا آلهة البحر، تُروى لآلاف السنين في
مجالس السمر حول النار. وقد تحولت كلمة لر لتصبح لير في تراجيديّة شِكسبير،
وسُمّي المكان الرئيسي لعبادته تيمُّناً باسمه: لِستَر (لر–سستَر).
إنّ قصة إطفال لر هي واحدة من المجموعة القصصيّة المُسماة "الأحزان الثلاثة في
تقليد سَرد الحكايات" وهي الأكثر رقة ومأسوية في كل الأساطير الكلتيّة.

Celts lived in Britain from around 700 BC. By 300 BC the Celts' lands extended from Ireland to Turkey.

The Celtic peoples of the British Isles were well-known for their love of story-telling, stories of Lir and his Family, Gods of the Sea, have been told around the fire for thousands of years. Lir's Welsh equivalent, Llyr, became King Lear in Shakespeare's tragedy, and the principal place of his worship was named after him: Leicester (Llyr-cester).

The Children of Lir is one of the *"Three Sorrows of Storytelling"*, in all of Celtic Legend there is no more tender or tragic tale.

English Pronunciation Guide:

Tuatha Dé Danaan	*Too-ha Day Dan-aan*	*Aoife*	*Ee-fa*
Fionnuala	*Fin-oo-la*	*Bodb the Red*	*Bov the Red*
Fiacra	*Fee-ak-ra*	*Sidhe*	*Shee*
Aed	*Ay (rhymes with day)*		

First published 2003 by Mantra
Global House, 303 Ballards Lane, London N12 8NP
www.mantralingua.com

Text copyright © 2003 Mantra Lingua
Illustrations copyright © 2003 Diana Mayo
This sound-enabled edition 2013
All rights reserved

British Library Cataloguing in Publication Data:
a catalogue record for this book is available
from the British Library.

أطفال لِر
The Children of Lir

Retold by Dawn Casey

Illustrated by Diana Mayo

Arabic translation by Dr. Sajida Fawzi

MANTRA
LINGUA

إستمعوا! سوف أقصُّ عليكم قصة أطفال لِر.

في قديم الزمان عندما كانت الأرض في بداية تكوينها وعندما كان السحر يلعب دوره دائماً، عاش في ذلك الوقت ملك اسمه لِر.

كان لِر ينتمي إلى تو-هادَي دان آن وهم قوم لهم خاصيّة الوهيّة حكمـوا أرض إرلندا الخضراء وكانت زوجة هذا الملك هي كُبرى بنات الملك الأعظم.

وقد أنعم الله عليهما بأربعة أطفال، ثلاثة أولاد وبنت واحدة اسمها فنؤولا. كانت فنؤولا هي الكُبرى ويليها آي ومن ثمَّ التـوأمـان الصغـيـران، فيـأكـرا وكُن. وأحبَّ الملك أَطفاله أكثر من أي شيء آخر في العالم وكانوا سُعداء لفترة من الزمن.

Listen! I will tell you the story of the Children of Lir.

Long ago, when the earth was young and there was always magic in the air, there lived a king named Lir.

Lir was one of the Tuatha Dé Danaan, the divine race which ruled over all green Ireland, and his wife was the eldest daughter of the High King.

They were blessed with four children: three sons and a single daughter, Fionnuala. Fionnuala was the eldest and next came Aed, and then the young twins Fiacra and Conn. The king loved his children more than anything else in the world, and, for a while, they were happy.

ولكن الملكة ماتت بعد ولادة التوأمين بفترة قصيرة. وحزن الملك عليها ، ولكن
الأطفال كانوا بحاجة إلى أم، فتزوج لِر إيفا، وهي الإبنة الثانية للملك الأعظم.
في البداية كانت إيفا حريصة ودائماً ضحوكة ونشيطة.
ولكنها بدأت تشعر بالغيرة حين لاحظت أنّ لِر
يحب أطفاله حباً عميقاً، فامتلأ قلبها
بالكراهية، وبدأت تمارس السحر سراً...

But soon after the twins were born the queen died. The king was
heartbroken, but the children needed a mother. And so Lir married
again, to the High King's second daughter, Aoife.
At first Aoife was caring, and always
full of life and laughter. But she saw
how deeply Lir loved his children,
and she grew jealous. Her light
heart grew heavy with hate,
and she began to practise
dark magic…

وفى صباح أحد الأيام، أيقظت الملكة الأطفال وأخذتهم
وهم لا يزالون في حالة نُعاس يتثاءبون،

إلى بحيرة نائية معزولة وقادتهم إلى الماء ليسبحوا.

"إسبحوا والعبوا، أعزائي"، قالت لهم بصوت رخيم وعذب كالعسل.

Early one morning the queen woke the children and led them, sleepy
and yawning, to a lonely lake, and sent them into the water to bathe.
"Swim and play, my dears," she told them, her voice as sweet and thick
as honey.

وفي الحال قفز الأطفال الثلاثة في الماء يتصايحون
ويصرخون ولكن فنئولا ترددت.
"إسبحي!" أمرتها الملكة. ونزلت الفتاة ببطئ إلى الماء.

The three boys splashed into the water at once, shrieking and
shouting, but Fionnuala hesitated.

"Swim!" the queen commanded. And slowly the girl waded into
the water.

راقبت فِنئُولا زوجة أبيها. واقشعر جسدها عندما رأت إيفا تسحب العصا السحرية من بين طيّات ردائها.

ورفعت الملكة ذراعيها وبدأت تُرتّل تراتيل هيبنوسيّة وسحبت العصا إلى الأسفل ولمست الأطفال واحداً واحداً على الحاجب.

وفي نفس اللحظة حلّ محـل الأطفـال فنؤولا، فيـأكرا، آي وكُن أربع بجعـات بيضاء جميلة تطفو على سطح الماء في نفس المكان الذي كان يسبح فية الأطفال.

Fionnuala watched her stepmother. The warmth drained from her body as she saw Aoife draw a Druid's wand from the folds of her cloak.

Raising her arms, the queen began to chant a hypnotic incantation, and she brought the wand down, touching the children, each in turn, upon the brow.

In an instant, where once Fionnuala, Fiacra, Aed and Conn had swum, there now floated four beautiful white swans.

"أطفال لِر"، بدأت إيفا ترتّل، "أرسل لعنتي عليكم! سوف تعيشون كبجعات لمدة ٩٠٠ سنة! يجب أن تقضوا في هذه البحيرة ٣٠٠ سنة و٣٠٠ سنة في البحر الإرلندي البارد وآخر ٣٠٠ سنة سوف تقضونها في المحيط الأطلسي الهائج".

إرتعب الأطفال ورفرفوا أجنحتهم حزناً وتأثراً متوسلين إليها أن تُخلي سبيلهم. ولكن الساحرة لم تفعل شيئاً سوى أنها ضحكت قائلة "لن يُخلى سبيلكم إلا إذا تزوجت ملكة من الجنوب بملك من الشمال وتسمعون دقات جرس معلنة عقيدة جديدة.

"Children of Lir!" Aoife intoned, "I curse you! You will live as swans for nine hundred years! You must spend three hundred years here on this lake, three hundred on the cold Irish Sea and the last three hundred on the wild Atlantic Ocean."

The children were terrified and beat their wings frantically, begging her to set them free. But the Sorceress only laughed. "You will never be free, until a queen from the South marries a king from the North, and you hear the sound of a bell ringing out a new faith."

"أوو إيفا"، توسلت فنؤولا بزوجة أبيها قائلة "لا تكوني قاسية جداً!"

فكرت إيفا قليلاً وتذكرت أنها كانت أماً لأطفال ورقّ قلبها قليلاً وقالت
"سيمكنكم الغناء بأصواتكم الحقيقية وستكون أغنيتكم هي أحلى أغنية سمعها
العالم".

وكان هذا هو آخر ما قالته الملكة قبل أن تغادر الشاطئ.

"Oh Aoife," Fionnuala pleaded with her stepmother, "do not be so cruel!"

Aoife paused, remembering how she had once been a mother to the children, and her hard heart softened a little. "You will be able to sing with your own voices, and your song will be the sweetest that the world has ever heard."

And with that the queen fled from the shore.

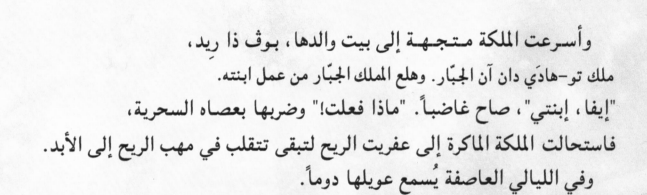

وأسرعت الملكة متجـهـة إلى بيت والدها، بـوڤ ذا رِيد،
ملك تو-هادَي دان آن الجبّار. وهلع الملك الجبّار من عمل ابنته.
"إيفا، إبنتي"، صاح غاضباً. "ماذا فعلت!" وضربها بعصاه السحرية،
فاستحالت الملكة الماكرة إلى عفريت الريح لتبقى تتقلب في مهب الريح إلى الأبد.
وفي الليالي العاصفة يُسمع عويلها دوماً.

She ran straight to her father, Bodb the Red, mighty king of
the Tuatha Dé Danaan. But the High King was horrified by his
daughter's deed. "Aoife, my daughter," he boomed, "what
have you done!" and he struck her with his Druid's wand.
The treacherous queen was transformed into a Demon
of the Air, to be tossed on the winds forever.

On a stormy night you can still hear her howls.

وبقي الملك لِر يفتش عن أبنائه في كل مكان، وعندما جاء إلى البحيرة ناداه الأطفال –
البجعات بإسمه وسمع لِر صوت أطفاله ولكن لم يرَ إلا بجعات بيضاء. ثمّ فهم الحقيقة
وكانت لحظة قاسية. وشعر بدموعه تنحدر على خدّيه عندما أسرع لِيحتضن أطفاله ولكنهم
لم يستطيعوا احتضانه حيث ليس لديهم أذرعة.

Meanwhile, King Lir searched everywhere for his children. As he came to the
lake the swan-children called out his name. Lir heard his children's voices, but
saw only four white swans. Then, in a terrible moment, he understood. The king
felt tears come to his eyes and they rolled down his cheeks as he rushed to
embrace his children, but, without arms, they could not hug him back.

ولاحظت فنؤولا القلق على وجه والدها ولأجل أن تهدأه بدأت تغني وشاركها إخوتها الغناء رافعينَ أصواتهم إلى السماء. آه! هذه الأغنية لها رِقة القمر. هذه الأغنية أرقّ من أي صوت إنساني وأحلى من كل أغاني الطيور.

وعندما سمع الملك العجوز هذه الموسيقى العذبة عاد الانتعاش إلى قلبه الحزين.

Fionnuala saw the anguish on her father's face, and longing to comfort him, she began to sing. Her brothers joined in, lifting their voices to the skies.

Oh! The silver of the moon was in that song. It was softer than any human voice, and sweeter than any bird song.

As the old king listened to the beautiful music his broken heart was soothed.

ويوماً بعد يوم كان لِر يأتي إلى البحيرة ليستمع إلى أطفاله – البجعات.

وذهب أيضاً إلى البَحيرة كل الـ-توهادَي-دان آن، وكل رجال إرلندة ليستمعوا إلى الأغنية الفضيّة الرقيقة.

وفُتن الناس في إرلندة بغناء أطفال لِر وبقوا مشدودين إليه لمدة ٣٠٠ سنة.

ولكن سرعان ما جاء اليـوم الذي كان يجب على الأطفال أن يغادروا والدهم وأهلهم ليذهبوا إلى البحر الإرلندي الهائج لإتمام الفترة الثانية من إبعادهم.

وطارت البجعات مغادرة إلى الشمال ولم يروا وجه والدهم مرة أخرى أبداً.

Day after day Lir came back to the lake to listen.

All the Tuatha Dé Danaan and all the men of Ireland went to the lake to hear the swans' silver song.

The wondrous singing of the Children of Lir held the people of Ireland entranced for three hundred years.

But, too soon, the day came for the swan-children to leave their father and their people, and to go to the angry Irish Sea, to fulfil the second period of their exile.

The swans flew north. They never saw their father's face again.

يمتد البحر الإرلندي بين إرلندة واسكتلندة، وهو بحر عاصب. إنه بحر مضطرب قارس البرودة ومعزول أيضاً. ولم يكن هناك من يستمع لغنائهم. وجمّدت الرياح القطبية ريشهم وكانوا يعانون لسعات الماء المتجمّد ويرتطمون بالصخور العتيدة.

The Irish Sea is a stormy stretch of water between Ireland and Scotland. A fierce and freezing sea it was, and lonely. There was no one to listen to their song.

There, arctic winds froze their feathers, and they were lashed by icy water, dashed against cruel rocks.

وإذا بعاصفة رعديّة تمرّ فوقهم في إحدى الليالي.

فكان عويل الرياح وصفيرها في كل مكان وكان الرعد يزمجر والبرق يشق ظلمة
السماء ولم يستطع الأطفال – البجعات مقاومة الرياح والأمواج التي ترطمهم،
فتفرقوا عن بعضهم البعض.

One night a terrible storm rolled in.

The wind howled and moaned, and thunderclouds groaned. Lightning
tore the sky. The swan-children were buffeted and flung apart by the wild
winds and waves.

وكان هناك صخرة واحدة فقط لا يتجاوز حجمها حجم رأس الفقمة استطاعت الصمود في وجه الأمواج المضطربة فحاولت فنؤولا التعلق بها وبدأت تغني كي يسمعها إخوتها حتى استطاعوا السباحة اليها بسلامة.

ولكن الأمواج المضطربة ارتطمت بالصخرة وبذلك ابتلّت أجسامهم بماء قارس البرودة.

فجمعتهم أختهم وضمّتهم تحت جناحيها.

فأدخلت كُون تحت جناحها الأيمن وفيـأكرا تحت جناحها الأيسر وآي الأخ الأخير وضع رأسه على صدرها.

Only one solitary rock, no bigger than a seal's head, rose above the crashing water. Fionnuala struggled to that rock, and sang out to her brothers until they crawled up to safety.

The pounding waves exploded against the rock drenching them with water, piercing cold, and they had to cling together to save from being washed away.

But the sister gathered her brothers under her wings and held them close, Conn under her right wing and Fiacra under her left, and the last brother, Aed, laid his head against her breast.

وانقضت ببطء ٣٠٠ سنة على وجودهم في ذلك المكان النائي، وأخيراً حان الوقت
لإتمام المرحلة الثالثة والأخيرة من دائرة السحر عليهم.

"يجب أن نذهب إلى المحيط الأطلسي"، قالت فِنؤولا لإخوتها. "ولكن في طريقنا
لنذهب ونحلّق فوق أرضنا لنرى والدنا".

وطارت البجعات خلال الليل وكانت أجنحتها تخفق سوية وتلمع تحت ضوء القمر.

Three hundred years passed slowly in that desolate place, but at last it was
time to fulfil the third and final stage of their long enchantment.

"We must go to the Atlantic," Fionnuala said to her brothers. "But on the
way, let us fly over our home and see our father."

The swans flew through the night, their wide white wings beating as one,
and shining in the moonlight.

وفي وقت مبكر تحت نور الصباح الباهت حلّقوا فوق الأرض التي عاشوا فيها طفولتهم ورصدوا الأرض من تحتهم على أمل أن يلقوا نظرة على قلعة والدهم. ولكن الموقع الذي كان يقوم فيه قصر لِر بروعته وجماله، لم يبق منه سوى أشواك في مهب الريح، فقد توفي والدهم منذ زمن بعيد.

فاستمرت البجعات في طيرانها وهي تغني لحناً حزيناً.

In the pale morning they flew over the land of their childhood, and scanned the ground, hoping to catch a glimpse of their father's fort. But where Lir's splendid palace had once stood, there was now nothing but nettles, blowing in the breeze. Their father was long since dead.

Keening a lament, the swans flew on.

وأخيراً وصلوا إلى شواطئ المحيط الأطلسي، وهناك وجدوا جزيرة صغيرة تسمى إينش كلورا. هناك وبعد تعب لوقت طويل، شعروا بالراحة ونعمت عظامهم بدفئ الشمس.

At last they came to the shores of the Atlantic Ocean, and there, they found a tiny island, named Inish Glora. Here, at long last, they rested. Once more they felt the gentle kiss of the sun, warming their bones.

وبقيت البجعات هناك تنتظر وتغني. وغنّوا الألحان التي تعلموها في أيام شبابهم
فتجمّعت في الجزيرة كلّ أسراب طيور اليابسة والبحر ليستمعوا مبهورين بغنائهم.

The swans stayed, waiting, and singing. They sang the Old Songs they
knew from their youth, and all the birds of the land and of the sea flocked
to the island to listen, spellbound.

وفي هذا المكان التقت البجعات – الأطفال بفلاّح شاب اسمه ايڤرك، الذي كان قد سمع قصّتهم وأخبر بها الآخرين. وهكذا بقيت قصّتهم حيّة ولا زلنا نقصّها نحن حتى اليوم.

لم يقابلوا أحداً لوقت طويل ومكثوا هكذا، حتى حضر إلى الجزيرة واحد من النسّاك.

وكان الناسك رجل دين ولكنه لم يكن من جماعة دان آن، حيث كان قد مضى ٩٠٠ سنة على الأقل منذ أن كانت فنؤولا وإخواتها أطفالاً.

قد تغيّرت الأمور الآن وأصبحت إرلندة الخضراء تحت حكم قوم جُدد، أما الأرباب القدماء قد اختفوا تحت الأرض وانتهى أمرهم كاسطورة.

It was here that they met the young farmer named Evric, who heard their story, and who told it. And so their tale was kept alive, and we tell it still today.

They saw no one else for a long time, until, one day, a hermit came to the island.

The hermit was a holy man, but he was not of the Danaan, for it was almost nine hundred years since Fionnuala and her brothers were children, and things had changed.

A new race now ruled the green lands of Ireland. The old gods had gone underground, transformed into *Sidhe*, Faery Folk, and faded into myth.

وكان الناسك قد سمع عن خبر أسطورة الملك لِر. وعندما سمع الألحان الأخّاذة للبجعات – الأطفال، تقدّم اليهم قائلاً "لا تخافوا"، "سأساعدكم أنا".

The hermit had heard tell of the legend of the Children of Lir. When he heard their enchanting music he approached them. "Do not be afraid," he said. "I will help you."

بنى الناسك كنيسة صغيرة في جزيرة اينش كلورا، وسمع أطفال لِر صوت رنين أجراس الكنيسة عبرَ الجزيرة.

وفي نفس الوقت كانت التحضيرات تجري في مكان بعيد لزفاف ملك من الشمال لملكة من الجنوب. وكانت هذه الملكة قد سمعت أيضاً حكايات عن البجعات المدهشة، وأحبّت أن تحصل على هذه البجعات، فطلبت من زوجها أن يقبض على البجعات ويقدمها كهدية زفاف لها. وهكذا خرج الملك لِيقبض على البجعات.

The hermit built a chapel on Inish Glora, and the Children of Lir heard the loud clear sound of a bell ringing, pealing out across the island.

At the same time, far away, wedding preparations were being made, for a king from the North was to marry a queen from the South.

This queen had also heard tales of the fabulous swans, and she wanted them for herself. She asked her new husband to get them for her, as a wedding gift, and so he set out to capture them.

وبطبيعة الحال رفض الناسك طلب الملك بالقبض على البجعات، ولكن الملك
حاول القبض عليها بشدة لغرض سحبها معه.

Of course the hermit refused him, but the king seized the swans
roughly, meaning to drag them away.

The moment the king touched the swans the spell was broken. The swans' plumage fell away, revealing, not the radiant forms of Danaan youths, but four shrivelled and wasted bodies, over nine hundred years old - three aged men and one ancient woman. As the feathers floated to the ground the last breath of life left their bodies.

وفي اللحظة التي لمس فيها الملك البجعات انتهى مفعول السحر.
وتساقط ريشهم ولم يظهر تحتها أجسام متألقة الشباب، كشباب قوم دان آن،
ولكنها كانت أجسام منكمشة وهزيلة يزيد عمرها عن ٩٠٠ سنة.
فظهر ثلاثة رجال طاعنين في السن وامرأة عجوز. وفي الوقت الذي كان
ريشهم يتساقط ويتراكم على الأرض كانت أجسامهم تلفظ أنفاسها الأخيرة.

"أدفنونا معاً في قبر واحد" قالت فنئؤولا.

وفعلوا كما طلبت. دفنوهم وفنئؤولا تضمّ كُون إلى يمينها وفيأكرا إلى يسارها،
بينما الأخ الأخير آي، كان مسنداً رأسه على صدرها.

وهكذا خَلُدَ أطفال لِر إلى الراحة الأبدية. ولكن، حسب ما يُقال، فقد ظلّ الناسك
حزيناً عليهم حتى نهاية حياته.

"Bury us together, in one grave," Fionnuala asked.

And so it was done. Fionnuala lay holding her brothers close, with Conn on her right, and Fiacra on her left, and the last brother, Aed, laid his head against her breast.

And so the Children of Lir found peace at last. But the hermit, it is said, sorrowed for them to the end of his days.